This book
belongs to

....

For Helen - the writer of letters,
the teller of family tales

A Random House book
Published by Random House Australia Pty Ltd
Level 3, 100 Pacific Highway, North Sydney NSW 2060
www.randomhouse.com.au

First published by Random House Australia in 2010

Addresses for companies within the Random House Group can be found at
www.randomhouse.com.au/offices.

National Library of Australia
Cataloguing-in-Publication Entry

> Author: Pelling, Lenny
> Title: Olden days / Lenny Pelling
> ISBN: 978 1 86471 902 4 (pbk.)
> Series: Pen pals forever; 3
> Target Audience: For pre-school age
> Subjects: Pen pals – Juvenile fiction
> Dewey Number: A823.4

Cover and internal illustration by Lenny Pelling
Cover design by Leanne Beattie
Internal design and typesetting by Astred Hicks, designcherry
Printed in Australia by Griffin Press, an Accredited ISO AS/NZS
14001:2004 Environmental Management System printer.

10 9 8 7 6 5 4 3 2 1

FSC
Mixed Sources
Product group from well-managed
forests and other controlled sources

Cert no. SGS-COC-005088
www.fsc.org
© 1996 Forest Stewardship Council

The paper this book is printed on is certified by the © 1996
Forest Stewardship Council A.C. (FSC). Griffin Press holds
FSC chain of custody SGS-COC-005088. FSC promotes
environmentally responsible, socially beneficial and
economically viable management of the world's forests.

Lenny Pelling

Pen Pals Forever

OLDEN DAYS

RANDOM HOUSE AUSTRALIA

Polly and Jez had written to each other about everything.

There was no secret they wouldn't share, no adventure they couldn't tell.

But every now and then, between chores on the farm at Glossop Downs or homework in the quiet streets of Mount Pleasant, even the best of friends sometimes run out of things to say.

The girls didn't have to look too far for inspiration. Polly's Gran liked nothing more than to spend an afternoon looking through her letters, pictures and diaries. She would stop every now and then with a faraway look in her eyes.

Polly tried to imagine what it was like
to live without computers and DVDs
and microwave popcorn.

Gran had travelled all around the world. When she'd met and married Pop, they had gone around it again together. At first, they had thought life on a farm might be a little too

quiet after the mountains and jungles and cities they'd seen. But in fact, this life was anything but quiet.

Jez couldn't talk to her grandmother about the olden days. Nanna June had passed away when Jez was very little. Even though Jez couldn't remember the last time they'd hugged or talked, she still felt like she knew her Nanna very well indeed.

Jez's Mum had kept all of Nanna June's treasures, photographs and letters safe in

her old tin trunk. When Jez or her mum missed Nanna June, they would spread them over the kitchen table and remember her together.

Dear Polly,

Last night, Mum showed me a photo of my Nanna June in Paris. I didn't know she had ever been outside Mount Pleasant but Mum said she and Grandpa went there for their honeymoon. They danced every night in the ballroom of their big hotel.

Love Jez

Polly danced until she was dizzy
enough to see two Red the Kelpies.

Dear Jez,
Today Gran and I found a letter
from my GREAT-grandmother! It
was written on the back of a pattern
for making dresses out of old
curtains and stuff. When she got
married, they didn't have enough
money for fancy clothes or wedding
cakes but it didn't matter.
Half the neighbourhood still came
to the party.
Love Polly

Jez

15 Wattle

Mount p

Jez wondered what kind of dress the shower curtains would make.

Dear Polly,

Mum showed me a newspaper cutout from the week I was born. Nanna June had written it to tell everyone that I had arrived. Mum said Nanna June was so proud she had even saved my baby shoes and the tooth I lost when I fell off my tricycle. I wish I had known her better.

Love Jez

Polly surprised Gran with a present to remember.

Dear Jez,

When my mum was even smaller than I am now, Gran and Pop took her climbing in the Atlas Mountains. The only atlas I've ever heard of is the biggest book at the library. Gran says the mountain kind grows out of the desert but still has snow on top.

Love Polly

Jez

15 Wattle Cre

Mount Pleasar

24

Jez planted a flag at the top of Mrs Formby's compost heap.

Dear Polly,

I found a certificate at the bottom of Nanna June's tin trunk yesterday. Did you know she was the first woman ever to finish the Tablelands Marathon? She came 78th in the end but Mum said she was so happy just to finish, she felt just like she had won it. They even gave her a blue ribbon!

Love Jez

Polly easily won the first ever Glossop Downs fun-run.

Dear Jez,
My gran was the first at something
too. She was the first to be arrested
at a protest march asking for equal
pay for women. Pop said he was never
prouder than when he went to pick her
up from jail.
Love Polly

Jez protested for equal time for girls
on the slippery-slide.

Dear Polly,

Today Mum and I remembered Nanna June's birthday by making her secret family recipe for triple berry scones with vanilla cream. It wasn't really a secret, though. Nanna June shared the recipe with everyone because she said it was the secret ingredient for a happy tummy.

Love, Chef Jez

Polly invented her own secret recipe
as a treat for Red the Kelpie.

Dear Jez,

Gran showed me her diaries from when she visited Brazil. She lived in a long hut with a family. They didn't have scones or cakes for tea. They didn't speak the same language, but they taught Gran how to make lunch from nuts and berries they found in the jungle.

Love Polly

Jez

15 Wattle Cres

Mount Pleasan

Jez had a tough time picking her favourite dish at lunch with her friend Lisa.

Dear Polly,

Long before Nanna June was a nanna, or even a mum, she went to college to be a nurse. One day she met a patient who had broken his leg in three places and needed her help just to get out of bed. It turns out the patient was Grandpa. He put up with hospital food, medicine and special exercises just to get to know her.

Love Jez

Polly couldn't think of anything
worse than catching boy germs.

Dear Jez,
When Pop was a soldier in Vietnam, he sent letters to Gran from the jungle written on anything he could find. He wrote on packets of oats and magazines with words I can't read, but every letter ends the same. *'Love always, your Cuddle-Monkey.'*
Love Polly

Jez

15 Watt

Mount F

Jez used her special jungle disguise to sneak up on Mrs Formby.

Dear Polly,

To celebrate the school's tenth birthday, my class buried a time capsule. Miss Milligan said that school kids years from now would be able to learn a lot from what we bury today. I put in a drawing of you and me and a letter from Nanna June. I hope those kids like triple berry scones with vanilla cream as much as I do.

Love Jez

52

Polly wondered which of her
treasures would outlast Red.

With the shearing over for another
year, it was time to head off in the
caravan again. There would be
no bedroom of her own for Polly,
but there would be plenty of new
adventures to tell and postcards and
emails to write.

Two generations, babies, computers and quite a few teeth later, Polly and Jez knew they had nothing to worry about. They would be writing to each other for a very long time.

PEN PAL TIPS

Scrapbooking with Polly

 ## Step 1

Start with a blank
scrapbook or journal
- you can even
decorate the
cover.

 ## Step 2

Try out different
themes before sticking
pieces down.

MY BEST FRIEND

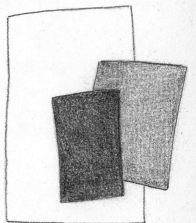

☀ Step 3

Try layering different coloured paper, textures, materials, ribbon or stickers - anything you like!

☀ Step 4

If you use acid-free paper, your creation could last a lifetime.

Sticky Dots

☀ Step 5

Use your imagination. What would you put in a time capsule?

PEN PAL TIPS

Write a postcard from the Olden Days

If you lived in another time, what would life be like?

✶ Would you go to school?

✶ Would you be a queen or a soldier or a jungle explorer?

✶ What would you do instead of watching TV or using a computer?

Make your own postcard! On a piece of
cardboard, draw your Olden Days adventure.

My Olden Days adventure

On the back, write a postcard from the Olden Days.

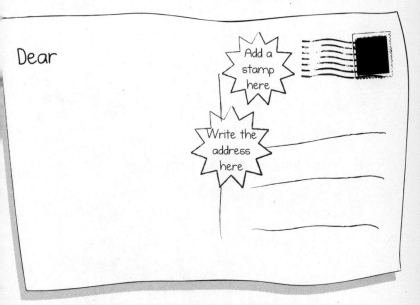

Dear

Add a stamp here

Write the address here